Five Mice and the Moon

Story by Joyce Dunbar
Pictures by James Mayhew

ORCHARD BOOKS

For Barbara Rock
J.D.
For my two grandmothers,
Joan Leighton and Beatrice Gibson
J.M.

ORCHARD BOOKS
96 Leonard Street, London EC2A 4RH
Orchard Books Australia
14 Mars Road, Lane Cove, NSW 2066
ISBN 1 85213 188 8 (hardback)
ISBN 1 85213 520 4 (paperback)
First published in Great Britain 1990
First paperback publication 1993

A CIP catalogue record for this book
is available from the British Library.
Printed in Belgium

Five hungry mice looked up at the moon.

One mouse said, "I am going to climb the tallest stalk in the barley field to see if I can *sniff* the moon. Then I'll tell you if it's really made of cheese."

"What a good idea," said the others.

They watched him climb the barley stalk, higher and higher and higher, until he clung to the very top.

"Are you sniffing the moon?" asked four hungry mice.

"No," said the mouse with a shiver.

From the top of the stalk
From where he stood
Can you guess what he spied
In the deep dark wood?

The snatching claws of a BADGER!
So he scurried off home as fast as he could.

Four hungry mice looked up at the moon.

One mouse said, "I am going to climb the tallest twig in the hawthorn hedge to see if I can *lick* the moon. Then I'll tell you if it's really made of cheese."

"How daring you are," said the others.

They watched him climb the tallest twig, higher and higher and higher, until he hung on to the tip at the top.

"Are you licking the moon?" asked three hungry mice.

"No," said the mouse with a tremor.

From the top of the twig
From where he stood
Can you guess what he spied
In the deep dark wood?

The wicked wet snout of a WEASEL!
So he scampered off home as fast as he could.

PRIVATE
KEEP OUT!

Three hungry mice looked up at the moon.

One mouse said, "I am going to climb the tallest post in the fence round the wood to see if I can *bite* the moon. Then I'll tell you if it's really made of cheese."

“Don’t break your teeth,” said the others.

They watched him climb the tallest post, higher and higher and higher, until he perched on the topmost tip.

“Are you biting the moon?” asked two hungry mice.

"No," said the mouse with a shudder.

From the top of the post
From where he stood
Can you guess what he spied
In the deep dark wood?

The fierce bright eyes of a FOX!
So he raced along home as fast as he could.

Two hungry mice looked up at the moon.

One mouse said, "I am going to climb the tallest tree that grows in the wood to see if I can *eat* the moon. Then I'll tell you if it's really made of cheese."

“Will you save a bit for me?” asked the other.

She watched him climb the tallest tree, higher and higher and higher, until he was right out of sight.

“Are you eating the moon?” called one hungry mouse.

"No," said the mouse in a flutter.

From the top of the tree
From where he stood
Can you guess what he spied
In the deep dark wood?

The sharp cruel beak of an OWL!
So he rushed along home as fast as he could.

One hungry mouse looked up at the moon.

She said to herself, "I am going to climb the picnic table in the clearing in the wood and I shall ask the moon to throw me down a piece of cheese."

So all by herself she climbed to the top of the picnic table which wasn't very high up at all.

"Please throw me down a piece of cheese," she said to the moon.

On the table top
In the clearing in the wood
Can you guess what she spied
From where she stood?

A great big slice of MOON CHEESE!

So she called to the others as loudly as she could.

Five hungry mice had a feast that night and they said, "Oh, the moon is lovely cheese."